Creston Books

Greetings, dear reader!
My name is
Lilliana Arianna de Darlingsweet-Amazingface!
But my friends just
call me LaDeeDa.
So you can too!

The Absolutely Positively NO Princesses Book

by Ian Lendler

Illustrated by Deborah Zemke

Hey! You! Didn't you see the title of the book?

NO princesses. You have to leave.

But...but everyone **adores** princesses!
Not me. Now out you go! And take this pink with you.
Take the pink? You can't be serious!
SHOO!

Sorry about that! Let me introduce myself. I'm Lita and this is my book. I love the outdoors, so we'll go into the wild, work with animals, and best of all, there will be absolutely, positively **NO—**

Yoo-hoo!

Aah! Why are YOU back?

Well, if you're doing a book, we should work on your outfit. I can help.

Princesses are good with outfits.

No way. I'm SICK of princess books.

All princesses ever say is ME, ME, ME and MINE, MINE, MINE. They're bossy and boring. So you have to go.

I'm not bossy. I'm just always right, so people should do what I say.

Look, do yourself a favor. At the very least, borrow my tiara.

Don't need it. I have a rubber band.

But you need me!
Your book needs flair!
Like this!
See, this is why I don't like princess stuff. Glitter in books always rubs off and makes a mess.

In my book, I hike into the forest and climb trees.
Ow! Oh! Do trees always have this many sticks?

Then, I'm going to work with animals on a ranch.
You realize we're standing in cow poo, right? I just want to be clear about this. You don't like glitter, but you have allowed a cow to poop in your book.

And my book will end around a campfire with a scary story. With bats and bugs and a mountain lion that eats princesses for lunch!
Ah! My wand! The lion chomped my wand!

Ahh! Why are you still here?!
I've decided a true princess can do anything she puts her mind to. And she can do it with flair! I'll show you!

Ever heard of a Rodeo Queen? Get along, little doggies!

As for scary,
I'll tell you a tale
of a fabulous
fire-breathing
dragon whose scales
are covered in rubies
and diamonds and
gold!

The Absolutely Positively ONE Princess Book

One princess? Hey! That's me!

Now LaDeeDa, these people have been waiting this entire time for us to tell a story.

Let's do it! What's this book about, anyway?

Cowboys?

Nah.

Princesses?

Nope.

Thank you, you're too kind! There are so many people to whom I'd like to dedicate this book. My parents, my manager, and of course, all the little people....

Okay, LaDeeDa, let them go. We hope you liked it, folks. Bye now!